I'll Take You to Mrs Cole

British Library Cataloguing in Publication Data
Gray, Nigel
   I'll take you to Mrs. Cole.
   I. Title   II. Foreman, Michael, *1938–*
  823'.914[J]   PZ7

ISBN 0-86264-105-5

First published in Great Britain by Andersen Press Ltd., 19–21 Conway Street, London W.1.
Published in Australia by Hutchinson Group (Australia) Pty. Ltd., Melbourne, Victoria 3122. All
rights reserved. Colour separated in Switzerland by Photolitho AG Offsetreproduktionen, Zürich.
Printed in Italy by Grafiche AZ, Verona.

10 9 8 7 6 5 4 3

I'll Take You to Mrs Cole

Text by Nigel Gray · Pictures by Michael Foreman

Andersen Press · London

When my mum came in from work
and I hadn't got the table laid,
she said,
"If you can't do what you're told,
I'll take you to Mrs Cole."

Mrs Cole lives down the street,
in a dirty house,
in a noisy house,
with lots of kids under her feet.

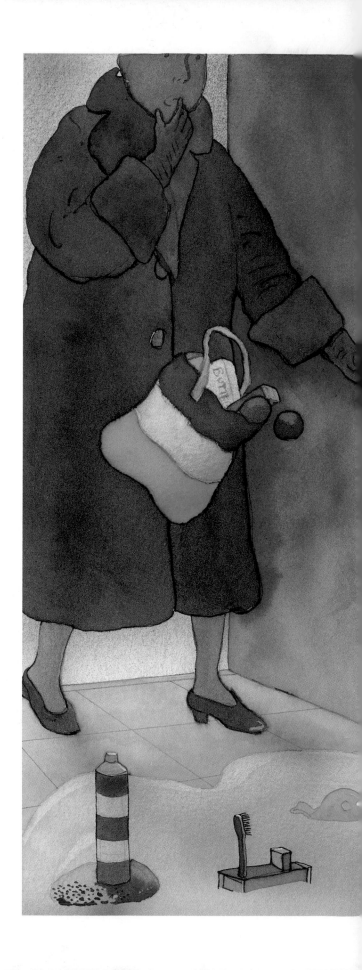

When my mum came in from work
and I'd been playing battleships
in the bath
and had flooded the floor of the flat,
she said,
"Put on your hat and coat.
I'm taking you to Mrs Cole."

I put on my hat and coat
and waited outside the door.
I wondered what it would be like
at Mrs Cole's.

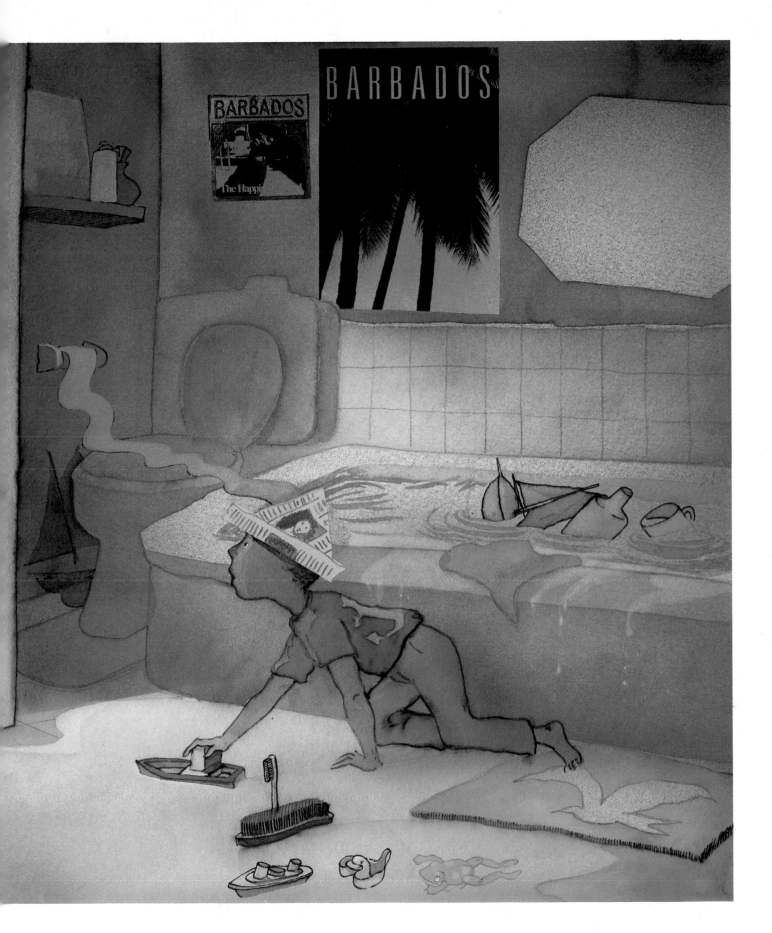

Perhaps her kids had no toys,
no clothes,
no telly,
no treats.

Perhaps she made them do
dusting and polishing and washing the floor
and whipped them when they fell asleep.

Perhaps she gave them
nothing to eat
except cabbage and curly kale.

Perhaps she kept them locked
in a dark and dismal dungeon
with green and slimy walls.

Perhaps she fed them to
her favourite pets:
boa constrictors,
alligators,
and piranha fish.

Then my mum told me
to take off my coat
and come back in.
"I'll let you off this time,"
she said,
"but next time you're bad,
I'll take you to Mrs Cole."

When my mum came in from work
and I'd broken the window
with my very bouncy ball,
she said,
"Put on your hat and coat.
I'm taking you to Mrs Cole."

I followed her down the damp dark street.
We crossed the road
and stood outside Mrs Cole's gate.
The lights were on all over the house.
There was music playing.
Thump, do-waddy-waddy thump.

I could see Mrs Cole inside the window.
She was fat and her face was red.
She had a baby in her arm.
She was stirring a wooden spoon
in a great big pan.
Round and round.
Round and round.
"Perhaps she's going to boil the baby,"
I thought.
"Perhaps she makes her children
into stew."

"All right,"
my mum said,
"I'll let you off this time.
Come on home with me.
But next time you're bad
I'm taking you to Mrs Cole."

Next day was Saturday.
My mum had to go to work.
"Do the washing up," she said.
"And make the beds.
Then get the shopping.
I've left a list.
And make sure the table's laid
before I get home for dinner.
And don't be doing any damage
or I'll take you to Mrs Cole."

After she'd gone
the flat was quiet,
and lonely,
and cold.
I looked at the dirty breakfast dishes
on the table.
I looked at the crumpled bedclothes
on the beds.
I decided to run away.

I went out into the misty morning street.
People bustled by with shopping bags.
No one noticed me.
A car drove through a puddle
and splashed dirty water up my legs.

I crossed the road.
I stood outside Mrs Cole's house.
The gate was hanging from one rusty hinge.
Weeds filled the front garden
taller than me.
It was like a jungle
from a Tarzan film.
The paint was scraped off the front door,
and there was a piece of cardboard
where the glass should be.

The lights were on all over the house
even though it was daytime.
There was music blaring out,
and a dog barking,
and children shouting.
Mrs Cole was still in the window.
I could see her making toast
and frying eggs,
and she still carried the baby
in her arm.
So she hadn't boiled it after all.

I stood waiting
on the grim grey street.
I wanted to run away.
But I didn't know where to go.
Then Mrs Cole came.

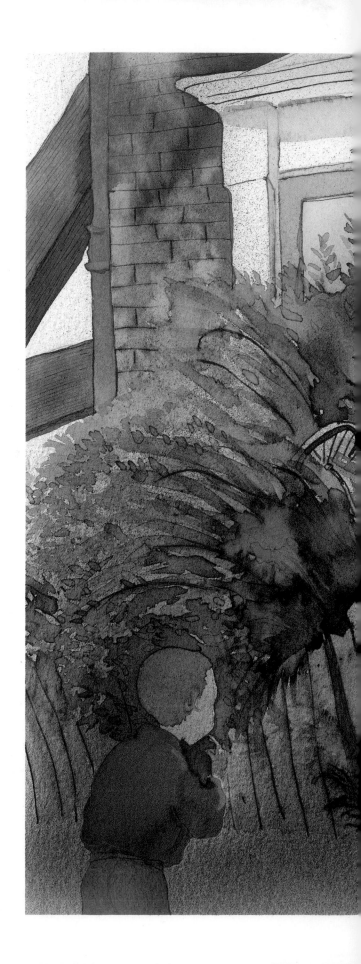

"Hello, me lover," she said.
"What are you doing in the cold
without a coat?
You'll catch your death."
She was big and red,
with straggly hair,
a scruffy cardigan,
and a great big smile.

"I'm running away from home," I said.
"Running away from home?" said Mrs Cole.
"Does your mother know?"
"No," I said.
"My mum's out at work."
"Well, you'd best come in, me lover,"
she said,
"and get warmed through."

I wondered if it was a trick,
if Mrs Cole was really
a child-catcher by trade,
and once I stepped inside
her smile would vanish
and a net would drop on me
from the ceiling,
and no one would ever know
where I'd gone.

But the street was cold.
Mrs Cole smelled of bacon,
and her house looked warm.
She took my hand
and we went inside.

In the hall
there was a pile of dirty washing,
a broken pram,
half a scooter,
a pyjama leg,
and three shoes:
one red,
one brown,
one blue.

In the kitchen
at the table
was a big boy
with a small boy on his head.

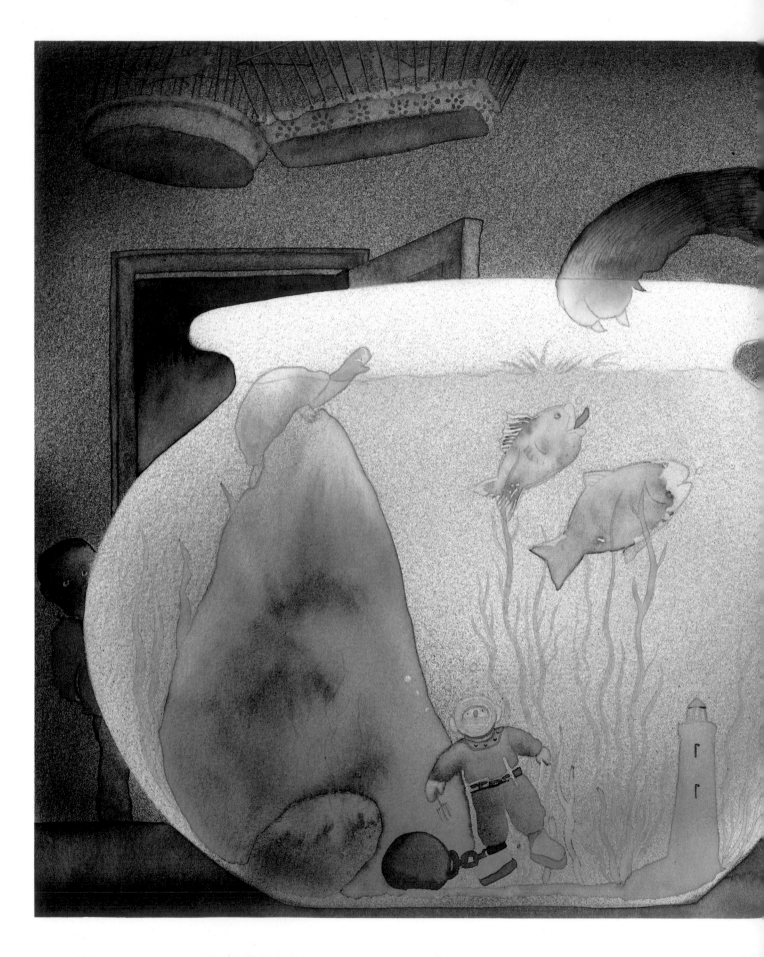

There were three cats
among the dishes on the table,
and one on the window-sill
who watched the goldfish
swimming in the tank.
A terrapin sat on a stone
and stretched his neck.

In the corner a black dog
lay dozing in a cardboard box
while four puppies
were feeding from her teats.

Two cages hung from the ceiling.
In one was a yellow canary who sang.
In the other,
two budgies,
one blue,
one green,
who chirruped and kisscd.

On an old settee
a girl and boy were eating toast,
talking with their mouths full,
and dropping crumbs.
But Mrs Cole
never told them off.

The baby lay on the settee
without a nappy on,
kicking its legs.
A little girl without any knickers
tottered around the kitchen floor.

The oven door was open,
and the oven was on
to make the kitchen warm.
Mrs Cole sang a song
with a singer on the radio,
and it didn't give her a headache.
She made me a bacon butty,
and a cup of tea.
"How many sugars?" she asked.
"Three," I said.
And she gave me three.
(My mum only lets me have one.)

"Mum," said the girl on the settee,
spraying crumbs all around the room.
"Polly's done a piddle on the floor."
Mrs Cole got a cloth
and wiped it up
and she never stopped from singing
the song she sang.

There was shouting and squealing
and bumping down the stairs.
A girl ran in
chased by a boy.
They fell in a heap
on the kitchen floor.

The girl shrieked,
"Mum! Mum! Michael's tickling me!
Stop him, Mum!"
"Leave her alone," said Mrs Cole,
"or I'll hold you down
and let her tickle you."

"But she won't feed the rabbits, Mum,
and they'll starve to death."
"It's not my turn."
"It is. It is."
"Well, me and Polly will feed the rabbits,"
said Mrs Cole,
"won't we, Polly, me lover,
and you two can do them tomorrow.
Today you've got a new friend to play with.
When he's finished his tea
take him with you,
and treat him nice."

I played all day.
And Mary and Michael
came and helped me do my housework.
When I was going home,
Mrs Cole said,
"Come back and play, me lover,
any time you like."

Nowadays my mum says,
"If you're good
you can go and play
at Mrs Cole's."
Because at Mrs Cole's,
they always treat me nice.